# BAND OF GOLD
## and Other Stories

## BOOK TWO OF THE
## KALEIDOSCOPE SERIES

**JULIE ROBERTS**
**Hartslock Publishing**

# BAND OF GOLD AND OTHER STORIES

Please note that the spelling and grammar in this book are UK English.

Published by **Hartslock Publishing**

# TABLE OF CONTENTS

WINGS OF LOVE............................ 5

ON GUARD.................................... 15

CORONER'S FOLLY...................... 18

THIS WAY, PLEASE....................... 26

ANIA............................................. 29

FENLANDS DAWN......................... 38

JORJA'S RESOLUTION.............. 43

THE DIARIES................................ 53

TURNING OF THE SEASON...... 56

ASK THE GREMLINS.................... 61

REVENGE...................................... 64

BAND OF GOLD............................ 77

SUNLIGHT TRAINING.................. 80

THE PROMISE............................... 93

ABOUT THE AUTHOR................. 101

EXCLUSIVE EXTRACT AND REVIEWS    103

## ACKNOWLEDGMENTS

I would like to thank Jeeve Publishing for their support. A special thank you to Nina Harrington for her help in getting this Kaleidoscope series into print.

---

## INTRODUCTION TO THE KALEIDOSCOPE SERIES

My Kaleidoscope series is a mixture of genres. As you turn the last page of a story, I hope you will find the change of lengths and emotions a pleasure to read. Or you may wish to hop around the pages at random. But whatever your choice, I hope you like what you find.

BOOK ONE – SILENT NIGHT *and Other Stories* –

available as an Ebook and paperback.

*Julie*

# WINGS OF LOVE

Kate pretended to read the newspaper headlines.

The next moment the offending broadsheet was snatched from her hands.

'Hiding from me isn't the answer, Kate. A husband has the right to know.' Babs pulled her from the kitchen chair and wrapped her in a hug. 'Keeping all this grief inside isn't doing you any good at all. You've got to tell Mike.'

Kate shuddered. 'I can't, Babs. Not with him in such danger in that Helmand Province.'

'Pumpkin, I know, but – '

'OK. A truce ... I will write.'

'Do it now. There's a note pad on the table.'

'No, after you've gone. I promise. As always, you're right.'

Babs nodded, kissed her cheek, stepped back and picked up her handbag. 'Mike loves you. Always remember that and all the rest will come out in the wash. I'll come over again in a few days.'

Kate closed the front door after her sister drove away. The hallway, the whole house seemed so hushed, as though it were holding its breath, waiting. Waiting as she waited, day after day, for ... but she couldn't let herself think beyond this moment. She pulled a chair from the kitchen table and sat down. She didn't want to keep her promise, but she had given her word. She thumbed the pen on and off, on and off. Her mind was full of the words she needed to say, then her brain sorted out the jumble and she started writing:

*My darling,*

*You are so far away. Yet when you phone you are here with me, your voice caresses my ear and your whispers of love make my heart beat faster. Then when you're gone I cry for the feel of your arms around me, your lips on mine ...*

Kate paused and drew the photo of Mike towards her. She'd taken it on his return from his previous tour of duty. They had gone to Wareham and she'd caught him, natural and relaxed at Corfe Castle amongst the ruins. He wore a navy shirt and white shorts, his skin tanned by the Afghan sun, his blonde hair bleached almost white. She picked up the frame and looked into his blue eyes, the corners creased with lines. They used to be laughter lines, or were they now from the harsh surroundings he had been stationed in? She kissed his picture and put it down.

*... Time seems to go very slowly, like the seasons. Remember when we walked through the bluebell wood, felt the warm sunshine through the trees. We sat on a patch of grass hidden behind the bushes on your old scout blanket that you insisted might come in handy one day. We ate our picnic, and made love. Springtime gifted us our most precious wish and when I told you, so many thousands of miles away that I was pregnant, we cried together, laughing that our tears could meet along that unseen beam that travels into space to connect us.*

*It's hard to tell you I've miscarried with our unborn baby. I want to comfort you as you read this; hold you close, kiss away our grief together. My voice is full of tears as I whisper, 'I want you darling, for you are the only one who can console me.' Babs has been so kind, but I want your words, not hers ...*

Kate stopped writing. Her hand was shaking so much she grasped her wrist to steady it, and then the last few days of pent-up emotions erupted with a flood of breathless, gulping tears that splashed and smudged her words on the page. Through the blur she pushed on her elbows and got up, her legs almost too weak to carry her to the sink to get a glass of water.

She splashed her face with cool water to sooth her eyes, then patted her face dry with a towel. She couldn't write again, not yet. Instead she ate a biscuit, washed and dried the glass, doing anything but pick up her pen. But it had to be done.

*... I hope there will be another time for us, but I am afraid you will not return to me. I should not be writing such fearsome words. But they are in my heart alongside my love. Somehow it's easier to write than say them to you.*

*I love you, Mike, with all my heart.*

*Kate xx*

She left the letter on the table and went to bed.

Kate woke and lay listening to the dawn chorus of the birds. Slowly sunlight filled the bedroom. The clock ticked past six o'clock. There was plenty of time to turn over and sleep for another hour, but the morning promised too beautiful a summer day to linger in bed. She showered, dressed and slipped a loose fitting pea-green sun dress over her honey-blonde curls. She rarely wore heavy makeup, just compact powder and pink lipstick. Mike called her his elfin wife when she wore green.

The letter lay on the kitchen table where she'd left it. Had she expected it to take legs and run away? That's what she wanted. She wanted everything to be as it had been three days ago. She wanted the morning sickness that had turned her into a wobbling jelly; she wanted only to be able to eat a slice of dry toast and drink a few sips of tea. Tears clogged her throat again and she swallowed, wiping her tears away with the tea towel. All she could think about was how she had felt: tired by eight each evening, the legendary cravings of Ryvita spread with marmite, cucumber sandwiches at dawn when she couldn't sleep. It was all gone, she was an empty shell. She now understood why the cow mooed for her calf when it was taken from her for weaning. Kate wanted to cry out too.

She picked up the letter, folded it and slipped it into the envelope. Her fingers gripped the pen very tight as she addressed it. Please don't hate me. Her plea ran round in her head and she did feel sick, but not the kind that she wished for.

The early evening sun played shadows with the kitchen cabinets.

'Did you send Mike a letter?' asked Babs. Then tilted her wine glass to make sure not a drop was wasted. 'I'm not sure that was the wisest way, but it's done. He had to know, Kate, it would have been wrong not to tell him.'

'How can you be so sure? What if he gets the letter just before a patrol? What if it troubles him so much he doesn't take care, doesn't concentrate on what he's doing? Oh, Babs...' Her voice trailed off and she picked up her wine and drank it all.

Her sister picked up the bottle and refilled her glass. 'No, dear, Mike is a professional soldier; he knows what he has to do.'

Kate got up from the table. 'Why are we sitting in the kitchen? This seems to be where I spend most of my life. Let's go for a walk.'

Behind the house a by-way crossed a field to a riverside path. They walked in silence; most of the regular strollers gone home to watch the television, or sipping cool lager in the local.

Kate picked a feathery dandelion and blew the seeds into the air. 'What if Mike doesn't come back ... I mean ... alive?'

'Of course he will, don't think like that.'

'I'll never have our baby; never have something of him to love.'

'Kate, that's enough. Dark thoughts will only upset you.'

'But I can't get it out of my head.'

Babs pointed to the pub garden that came into view round the bend. 'Shall we have a drink? A little nip to calm the nerves.'

'I don't know ... OK, just a small one.'

Kate chose a garden table close to a highly scented rose bed. She breathed in deeply, closed her eyes, and said, 'Mike hasn't phoned. Do you think he's all right?'

'Yes, I do.'

'He may be away from the base. He won't know yet. My letter is just waiting there.'

'You're getting all worked up again. Look at that sunset, Kate? Isn't it beautiful?'

Kate looked beyond Bab's waving arm. The sun was low, turning the sky into a streaked skein of orange, red and purple. The calling of the birdsong gradually lessened as the dusk deepened and the river became a moonlit path winding away into the distance.

'Thank you for coming this evening, Babs. I was feeling really lonely tonight.'

'I'm always here for you little sister, even if you do try my patience at times.'

'Sorry about that. Shall we wander back? I don't really feel like drinking.'

'We may look like sisters, Kate, petite and blonde, but you've got Dad's ways and I suppose I've got Mum's. But I think the resemblance ends there. You're strong, even if you don't see it. Being a soldier's wife takes a lot of courage, especially in these troubled times. Me, I plumped for the easy life with Ted and his local government job. Don't you ever forget that! I never let anyone forget how my little sister copes with months alone, works far too many hours a week at that advertising agency, and runs the Girl Guide group. Walk tall Catherine Jane, life will get better again.' She took hold of Kate's hand and squeezed it tight. 'It's getting chilly and I didn't bring a woolly.'

'Thanks, big sister, I know you're right. Let's go home and have a coffee, then I'll let you go home to that husband of yours. Give Ted a hug for me and tell him he has a very grateful sister-in-law.'

Kate could hear the phone ringing and fumbled for the receiver on her bedside cabinet.

'Hello?'

'Kate?' Mike's voice sounded strained.

'Oh, Mike, is that you?' And she burst into tears.

'Darling, please don't cry. Everything will be all right. Why didn't you go to the Adjutant's Office?'

'Oh, I know I should, but I just couldn't. Babs said –'

'Never mind that now. What has the doctor said? Shouldn't you be in hospital? What am I thinking of? How are you, my love?'

'OK, I suppose. Oh, I need you so much.' Kate struggled to control her voice, get it back to some sort of normality. 'Sorry, I'm just emotional at the moment. How are you? Have you been out on patrol? The news is nothing but bombs and death; I can't bear to hear it any more.'

'Shh. I'm all right, Kate.'

Just all right? She had to live each day not knowing if that knock might come – and like an echoing thought the doorbell rang. Her heart started to hammer, taking her breath away. But it wasn't the dreaded caller, Mike was talking to her, Mike was alive.

'There's someone at the door. It'll be the postman. He can leave what he's got on the step.'

'I think you should go and open it.'

'But I'd sooner –'

'It may be important. I can wait.'

Kate pushed the duvet back and raced down the stairs. What could he be delivering? She wasn't expecting anything, except bills. Throwing the door open Kate stopped and mumbled some unintelligible, 'But, what, Mike?' There was no short, tubby postman. It was her tall, blonde, very tired looking husband leaning on the doorbell.

'Hi, sweetheart – a special delivery with the compliments of the Royal Air Force,' and he scooped her into his arms.

Kate was, at last, where she needed to be.

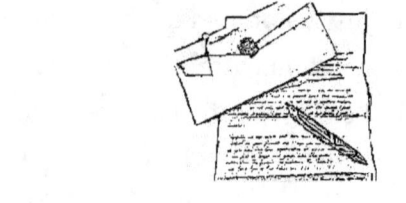

# ON GUARD

**1.30pm**

The wooden chair was placed in the centre of the room. There was a slight moulding for the posterior and a slatted back to hang the shoulder blades on.

**1.35pm**

Maud Jenkins sat down.

She shifted her weight. It was a chair designed to be uncomfortable, to keep the sitter awake. Her eyes looked at the clock, watching the minutes tick by.

Behind her, Charles grunted, snorted down his nose and moved his head from side to side in the winged chair. His feet were propped on a footstool. He looked really comfortable.

Opposite Charles, Beatrice and George sat together asleep on the paisley sofa. She whistled like a branch-line steam train and he overtook her with his main line rattle. They were like the rain and shine weather people that hung in the hall.

**1.45pm**

The clock chimed.

**1.50pm**

Maud stretched her legs and arched her back. It was only fair she took her turn, but she was bored and that made her eyelids droop. As she slipped sideways the corner of the chair back dug into her spine. There was no chance of having forty winks on this!

Primrose fidgeted in her sleep, sighing every few seconds. Her thin claw-like hands plucked at her skirt. Did that mean a good or bad dream?

Maud took another look at the clock.

The overture of snores was like an orchestra tuning up, minor and major notes not in harmony.

**1.55pm**

Maud reached over to the portable radio and pressed the button.

Eighty decibels blasted out. The snoring stopped. Heads came up. Bodies straightened. Hands moved to take the cups of cold tea.

**2.00pm**

Two chimes resonated from the mantel clock.

Hearing aids were adjusted, eyes focused on the radio set and the theme tune of The Archers rang out.

Maud rose and went to sit in her comfortable chair. It would be another fortnight before she was on guard duty again.

# CORONER'S FOLLY

The crematorium curtains closed on the coffin.

Fiona Marshall let 'crocodile tears' run down her face and dabbed her nose with a hanky. The hand that held it had a silver ring embedded in the flesh on her middle finger. She stood up, noticing as usual, that she took up twice the space of anyone else. When had she become jealous of her sister? Probably when she realised how different they were. Over the years, envy had festered into obsessive jealousy. She was free from all that now and could begin her new life.

\* \* \*

The recorded male voice; heavily accented and with a wheezy rattle, said. 'I took your book.' That was all, and the answerphone clicked off.

In the silence, Fiona stood as though carved in stone, her face drained of any colour and her blue eyes full of fear. If the foreign man was the burglar who had entered her cottage a few days ago, he must know her secret. She forced unwilling feet to move over to the cabinet and with trembling hands searched the drawer. The journal was gone. She hadn't reported the robbery to the police, because she thought he had taken only worthless ornaments.

The phone rang and she jumped like a frightened rabbit.

'Fiona. It's the vicar. I was clearing out the dead flowers bin and found a book belonging to you. It has your name on the cover.'

How was this possible? It contradicted the phone call. 'Yes ... I lost it a few days ago. Are you still in the churchyard? I'll come now and collect it.'

'Yes, I am. It's a lovely evening; I'll wait on the seat under the oak tree.'


Fiona was panting when she sat down next to the vicar.

'Thank you,' she said, as he handed her the precious item.

'You're lucky it's my turn for clearing up this week, old Jack Filey's almost blind.'

'Very lucky, vicar.' Very, very lucky, she thought, as she put the book in her pocket.

They sat together, quietly looking at the ancient, discoloured headstones with the evening song of the birds filling the air. The vicar sighed and turned to the woman who had taken over Jeffrey Cooper's law practice, 'How is the business going?'

Under a mass of blonde frizzy curls, Fiona grimaced, but her blue eyes sparkled, 'As well as can be expected. Teaching a dinosaur secretary the ways of the space age is taking time, but the clients are coming in. What more can I ask?' Her smile turned a pale face into a picture-book full-moon.

The church bells began to ring.

'Tuesday practice has started. I must go.'

The silver haired vicar limped away, leaning heavily on his walking stick.

Fiona heard the phone ringing as she walked up the garden path, but it stopped before she opened the door.

His voice was there again on the answerphone. 'I've kept the page.'

He was playing cat and mouse with her. How long before he mentioned money?

The sitting room darkened and Fiona nestled deep into the settee cushions. She opened the journal and ran a finger up and down the jagged page edge, waiting for another call. She turned on the television, and jumped each time a phone rang from the screen. When she went to bed, she laid awake and plotted ways to flush him out. Dawn light was colouring the sky when the phone finally rang.

'I want five thousand pounds, in used fifties, by tomorrow.' The croaking voice was so bad she wasn't sure she had heard correctly and shouted, 'What do you want? I can't understand you.' The voice repeated it slowly and ended the call.

So, it was definitely blackmail – big time.

This was madness, but she needed that page back. Payment was the only way. If five thousand was all he wanted, so be it, but if this was the first of many ... she didn't have a bottomless pit of cash ... pay this time and see what happens.

The following evening she arrived home and saw the answerphone light flashing. There was only one message and his disgusting voice said, 'Put the money on the grave of Henry Fowler. It's in the middle row opposite the oak tree. At midnight. Not a moment before. Go straight home. I will know if you disobey me.'

There was no mention of the torn-out page. How was she going to get it? Would he post it to her, or phone, saying where she could find it? She shouldn't part with the money until she knew, but if she didn't pay what would happen?

In the moonlight, the granite church had taken on a silvery gossamer cloak and the clock hands were almost together on the twelve. The grass was damp and she stumbled over clumps of moss; the tombs' engravings were difficult to read in the penlight, but she found the grave and drew a package from the inside of her coat. She hesitated, reluctant to leave the money without knowing when she would receive the page. Was there honour amongst thieves? She hoped so. Had Henry Fowler been a thief? Would his ghost, if it were around, make sure the wheezy blackmailer kept his word? 'I leave this package in your keeping, Henry, don't let me down.'

There was no post or telephone call.

Fiona, feeling like a pendulum, swung between hope and despair.

On the third evening the phone rang.

'It isn't quite enough, dearie. My expenses have risen, I need another five thousand.'

The rattling breath raced through her ear channels into her brain. 'I haven't any more money; you've had all my savings. This wasn't the agreement; I want the journal page back, now.'

'A final payment, dearie, or I will send it to the police.'

'How do I know you'll keep your promise?' Fiona's head was hammering and she couldn't get enough air into her lungs; pins and needles were stinging her hands and her legs were sagging. She saw black blotches before her eyes.

'You'll have to trust me, dearie. Five thousand, same place tomorrow night.'

Gulping in air, she whispered, 'I need to meet you this time. Be at Henry Fowler's grave. No page. No payment.'

'OK. Until tomorrow, dearie.'

The phone line went dead and Fiona sank to the floor, trembling from head to toe.


Wheezy Voice didn't come the next night and Fiona went home feeling both relief and dread. She knew the blackmail ruse was not over. Did he fear her seeing him? That she would recognise him? But maybe she could turn the tables, exert pressure to force a meeting on her terms, a place and time of her choosing – a dark night, a canal lock. As the plan rolled around in her mind the phone rang ...

Deep in the countryside, far from human habitation, Fiona stepped from the towpath into the shadow of the bushes. She pulled on a pair of gloves, pushed the leather down tight over her fingers and crossed her arms under the overdeveloped bosom.

A few minutes later, a short figure in a long overcoat approached the lock. Any shape or disability that could identify him was hidden and a balaclava, slit at the eyes, covered his head and face. He stopped by the lock gate beam, twisting his head like an owl looking for a meal.

As she stepped forward a twig snapped and he turned round.

Fiona's hatred for this man spewed out. 'Have you got the page this time?' She wanted to push him, but she understood the need for patience. It was a lawyers' rule.

He fumbled in his coat pocket and brought out a sheet of paper, handed it to Fiona. In the light of her torch she saw it was the original page. She zipped it into her anorak pocket. 'Have you made copies of it?'

'No. Why should I? Ten thousand suits my needs. I can always find another sucker to fleece.'

Now was the moment!

The splash sounded very loud in the stillness of the night. His arms beat the water, he spluttered through his clogged throat and nostrils as the sodden overcoat dragged him down. It was all over in a few minutes.

The moon slipped from behind water-laden clouds and illuminated her face. A smile of pleasure parted her lips and she said, 'Death by misadventure.'

The cottage light shone like a beacon in the darkness. Inside, Fiona sat cross-legged like a Buddha on the king-size bed carefully taping the missing page back into her journal. She smoothed the creases and read the words – I killed my twin sister.

She picked up a framed newspaper cutting from the bedside table. It showed a tall, slim woman in a swimsuit. Her oval face was flawless with arched brows above almond shaped eyes. Flowing blonde hair cascaded down over her bare shoulders and seawater sprayed, as she skied behind a motor-boat under a clear sky. High rise apartments in the background shouted French Riviera – the models' photo shoot paradise. The caption read:

*'Angela Marshall – Coroner's verdict – Accidental death'*

Fiona poked her tongue out at the photo. In a spiteful tone she hissed, 'Slim bitch.'

Although becoming a double killer had not been her intention.

# THIS WAY, PLEASE

In a convoy of traffic driving along the M4 towards the Severn Bridge, I could have been classed as a car-and-a-half. The wind blew a near hurricane and the rain was coming down like stair-rods.

Ahead of me, soaked to the skin, Tony was riding his 1961 Norton motorbike.

My car's 'half' was the trailer towing Horace, his 1934 Royal Enfield.

What a night to have come out. We should have waited until morning. But it was too late for 'if only' thoughts.

The one not vexed was the circular cushion of ginger and white fur curled on the passenger seat. From time to time his paw twitched – probably dreaming of mice.

Out of the darkness a warning sign flashed: the bridge was closed to high-sided vehicles and caravans.

This wasn't for me. My little trailer didn't come under this order.

As the miles decreased, the warning signs appeared again.

Not for me, mate. I'm going across the bridge.

What's that up ahead? It looks like a queue of traffic. I don't need this. I'm tired and this awful weather is straining my eyes.

There's a policeman waving a torch. Why? He's turning the high sided lorries and caravans off down the slip road just before the bridge. That means they have to go the long way round, up to Gloucester.

Hell's bells!

What's he doing, waving me off! I've only got a little motorbike on the back.

OK, OK.

Let's pretend.

If you think I'm going via Timbuktu, you have another thought coming. There's plenty of room between the cones for my little car to get back through!

What's wrong with this? I'm crossing the bridge fine.

I wonder where Tony is. I haven't seen him for ages. He disappeared into the darkness miles back.

I hope he's waiting for me on the other side, I don't know the way to Whitecroft. I don't have a map.

Do you want to know what happened?

Knowing that trailers were being turned off, he was waiting for me down at the roundabout below the bridge. He watched me go driving across.

I won't print what he was calling me. Just to say, he crossed the bridge on the cyclists' path!

Abandoned, I drove purely from what I had seen on the map days before. And we both arrived at the campsite within ten minutes of each other.

How's that for dead reckoning navigation?

# ANIA

I kneel here on the harbour cobbles, praying for my husband's return. I have not given up praying and begging to God that He has saved our fishermen from the mighty storm and sent their fishing boats home. The other wives have stopped coming. I cannot, for without his return I must do something that will break my heart.

There have been seven days of dark skies but tonight the sky is clear and the stars bright. The moon is full and by its light I can see the tide rising on the great Tiber.

The harbour has an unnatural look – it is empty – only the sound of rowing boats tied to iron rings, tap the wall as the water surges into the bay. The water is black and sinister, like a cloak hiding everything below, hiding the fish and crabs the boys catch to feed the widowed women – of which I may be one now. But this is not enough; we need our men to return. He must come back.

Do my eyes deceive me; is the power of my desire so great that I can see phantoms? No. A fleet is coming in – the second fleet – have they found our men? My hands are shaking and my fingers hurt, for I am squeezing them together in homage to my God. Yet I cannot say the words until I see my Mario step ashore.

The boats are riding swiftly on the tide. Some will moor alongside the wall and others in the harbour. Should I run and tell the women? No! I will wait for my Mario, he may be hurt, may need my help. They should be here, praying as I am. They must hear the sound of the oars, the voices shouting out the orders to heave-to.

The first boat alongside is Crispin's. He does not look triumphant. There are many men, more than the one crew. Does that mean he found them? Found them in that mountainous sea where the waves ride high above their boats when the storms are upon us. I can't see in the dark how many boats are coming in. The second fleet has five and the first fleet seven. There should be twelve. I cannot see how many, my eyes are misty with tears. The plank is coming over the side.

Torchlight is coming from the town. They have been woken by the noise. The old men are hobbling; the young racing in front and the mothers holding their children by the hand. I can see my sister, Beatrice, with her babes and mine. Hurry them fast, they must be here to welcome their father.

Marcus and Lavia, my children, are with me – waiting and hoping for a miracle. One by one the survivors are coming ashore. Their clothes are in tatters and many have bandages over their eyes, for when sea water slaps into them they become very sore. Two of Mario's crew, Leo and Felix, have bandaged hands, probably full of splinters and some truly unfortunate souls, have twisted limbs. They will never sail again. It will be difficult for them to find work. Cripples are not looked upon with any favour. They will end up beggars and their women-folk, whores.

My Mario is not with them.

They could not find him in the sea. Seven boats sailed – none have returned. Seven hauls of fish lost. A good catch will feed the fleet and what's left is dried and smoked; the women sell it in the markets of Ostia.

I am a true widow now.

Beatrice has tried to console me, but she has her husband, a second fleet fisherman to comfort, and two small babes hanging on her skirt to nurse. I must go now and take my children to our home. They are but five and four years old and do not understand my grief. I must be strong and not break down until they are bedded. Then I can cry silent tears in the bed Mario and I shared; where he whispered, 'Cleo, my dearest.' And I opened for his love.

They are asleep. I told them that their father would not be returning from the sea, that God had need of him in heaven. Neither child seemed to understand, perhaps because they were so tired. I'm sure in the morning they will have many questions.

Our one room is curtained in half – for sleep and to live. Mario made a window, so that I might sit and look at the countryside. I often dream of living in the villa I can see, owned by the Overseer. In the heat of summer, I imagine my bare feet walking on marble floors and cooling my fingers in a courtyard fountain. But at this moment, I sit here and watch the peach paleness of the dawn bring colour to the green shoots of corn, rising straight like sword tips from the ground. Hedges are showing buds and, far away in the distance, hills have a purple tinge. I want to sit here forever, watch time go by and not have to worry about what I am going to do. There is our hidden box, but that was always meant for when Mario could not sail anymore, when he was old. He is never going to grow old – I will only remember him as my dark-haired, handsome husband with his sunburnt skin a little lighter than the colour of his boat.

I need something of his to hold. There is his shirt on the line. It was Mario's favourite – grey, woven thick cloth. It has a dark hair caught in the open neckline. I shall never see him in it again, never touch his dark hair and never kiss his lips. How am I to bear the pain of losing him? And without him, how can I care for another child, for it is surely coming within a few days.

I can hear the children are awake. They will come to me now for their breakfast. But this day will be different – it is a day of mourning.

Marcus is very like his father; decisive, forceful and the most handsome boy a mother could wish for. He is my first born and I am so proud of him. He is standing with his feet apart, hands behind his back, just like Mario, and has a quiver in his voice. He is declaring that he will look after me and Lavia. He will go fishing with the boys and bring home our food. I can work in the fish smoke rooms and his sister can sweep the floors. He must be so frightened. But I must not show any compassion. I must bow my head and agree.

Little Lavia is staring at him with wonder in her face. Compliance from her is something to behold. She is like me with her fiery temper, dark hair and olive skin, a true descendent of Latium.

It is time – time for me to go into the woods and prepare my place. I have what I need: cloths, knife and blanket. I asked Beatrice to care for Marcus and Lavia, yet not my reason why. She would want to come with me, but I do not want that. This will be a time for me and Mario – me and his memory. I have borne two children, I am not a novice. Yet if anything goes wrong, my babes will become orphans. Children left to be cared for by Beatrice, who could not cope with such a burden. Black thoughts are not for now – I must be strong like my little Marcus – take the responsibility into my hands.

The afternoon is paling. There is no trodden path where I am walking. The Tiber is wide and fast flowing, but soon I shall see a backwater, thickly surrounded by trees and cut by a small island. It is an ideal place for me to make a shelter.

The twigs are burning and the fire is giving good warmth. Mario and I did this when first married, when we were free to run, laugh and love in a bough shelter under the stars. I love him so much. Is his memory enough for me to brave this alone – to give birth? It is, for it will be his hands that rub and ease my pain, his voice will be in my head, encouraging, telling me when the time is right. And the time is now – the first pain has begun.

I see it come as the dawn lightens my shelter. Its cry fills the air. It is a girl. I must rest for a few moments, but when I tend to her and myself, I will count her fingers and toes.

She is beautiful, only her face shows from the blanket. I want to cradle her forever. I want to remember every moment that Mario and I shared when we joined to create such a wonder. He is here, beside me, so vivid and real – yet nothing more than a ghost that must fade before the sun sets tonight.

The fire needs more twigs. 'Mario, can you put them on.' His hands through mine coax the fire for more warmth and I lay down to sleep with Ania – the girl name we chose many months ago.

The sun is well into the heavens and it is Ania's cry that has woken me. She must be hungry and I have my milk for her now. The fire has gone out, but the air is warm and we are not cold. Come little one, it is time to fill your need.

I walk in the woods, telling her all about her father, Marcus and Lavia. I show her the trees and the river where the fish run deep and are not easy to catch. I keep telling her how much I love her. But the time has come to go and say goodbye to where much love has been shared.

I kneel and give prayer. 'Oh God, it is with great sorrow that I pray to You now. But, also, it is with great gratitude that I bless our beloved Pope Innocent III, who has, in his wisdom, made it possible for me to place Ania in his care. I give her to you with my love.'

The water is cold, but I must do this, for Mario and me. 'Do not cry, little one, it is only for a few moments. I ask, O Lord, for your blessing and name this child, Ania. She will have no other name. Amen.' The water is dripping onto her blanket, but the cross is there on her forehead. 'You have been baptised, my dearest daughter, in the Christian faith.'

The drinking houses are closed. The town is asleep. A few dogs are growling. I creep in the shadows, peer round corners. I have not seen anyone that could be a danger to us. My weakness is making me tremble and I have a sweat on my forehead. Mario would not have let me get up so soon, but I must do this, before I change my mind. It is not what I want. I want to keep her, suckle her and love her. But we would not survive – Marcus cannot fish and Lavia cannot sweep floors. We have only what money is in the box and I can work with only two little ones to care for.

I am here. The convent gates are unlocked, and the foundling wheel is there in the wall, as His Holiness deemed it to be.

The box is small. She looks so beautiful. I must close the lid and turn it inside. 'Goodbye, my sweet Ania. I pray the nuns will care for you as I would.'

It is done.

My heart will hold you both forever.

'Goodbye, Mario, until we meet again.'

# FENLANDS DAWN

*A story inspired by a painting*

Below the Eastern horizon dawn was breaking with a wash of yellow light. As the earth rolled, the sun rose into the sky illuminating a lone Mosquito aircraft flying above the North Sea, homeward to the coast of England.

The port engine spluttered, died, and three propeller blades appeared in the invisible circle of air.

The plane lurched and Gus looked out of his cockpit side window. Through clenched teeth he muttered, 'son-of-a-bitch, not now, you're a tricky bird on two engines, one you're a flying beast.'

He raised his right arm, seeing it tremble as he reached for the control to feather the blades and adjust the trim. His feet didn't want to move, they had turned into lead weights as he held them on the rudder pedals.

Gus hunched his shoulders, hoping to ease the pain in his chest. He looked down at the trickle of blood that was seeping through the zipper of his flying-jacket. Drop by drop it splashed onto his thighs.

His left arm was extended like a stick and the gloved fingers held the control column in a death grip. He was a mess; a cramped hurting body being forced by his brain to its demand that he get his Mossie back in one piece.

He was cold, yet he could feel sweat dripping off the ends of his dark hair on to his forehead and run down his face. He glanced in the mirror that he had glued to the flight panel. He was 23 and he looked like his grandpa – old, gaunt and ashen.

Pain made his eyes water as he searched the instruments. The old bird was almost out of gas, it must have been some Jerry's wild cannon fire to make this bitch leak. Could he coax the last few gallons to make the airfield?

Out of the sea land mapped into the Norfolk Fens. Water channelled into arteries, then as veins criss-crossing the marshland. Reeds swayed with the morning breeze.

Gus's vision blurred, he blinked. He had to keep alert to maintain a steady descent, follow the river to turn at Little Willow village for the airfield. Glancing over his right shoulder, the holes in his navigator's side window whistled notes of inharmonious music, lifted the corners of the pages on the clipboard clutched in his friend's hand, his staring eyes lifeless.

'Hell, Jack, what a night. I know you can't hear me, but I have to talk to someone. I need you to help me stay conscious, just listen to me. Berlin...'

The live engine spluttered for a few seconds, then picked up again. Gus looked at the fuel gauge and closed his eyes.

'... Berlin was an inferno, a roaring bonfire. Those blast bombs annihilated the buildings, the factories, the homes. But Jerry's searchlights and gunners picked the squadron out easily. They knew the raid was coming. We were okay until that flak on your side. Heck, boy, I'm sorry, but we'll make it. Hold on to your spirit till we land. Then you can fly to heaven and home to Kansas.'

The photo, pinned to the billet room wall, filled his mind: Jack, the typical farm boy with Lisa, her unborn child showing beneath her summer dress. Her chin tilted, her eyes looking into his.

Gus's guilt engulfed him. It was a pilot's job to look after his crew.

The fuel needle dropped to zero. Their luck had run out.

Adrenaline pumped through his body. His right arm was as stiff as a broomstick and he cried out, 'Move, damn you,' forcing it upwards to press his mike button.

'Charlie Baker One, almost out of gas. Need help now. Crew injured.'

White noise hissed in his ear, snaked along the nerves in his head.

Then a female voice called clear, and precise. 'Charlie Baker One. Clear to land. Approach is dead ahead, three miles. Runway lights on. You have a green. Good luck!'

Was he that close to base?

'Where are you? I can't see the airfield.'

Panic welled within him. His head pounded, his throat contracted. Through the splintered window was only golden wheat. It spread like his mother's comforter. A warm bed, a place to sleep, he was so tired.

'Charlie Baker One...'

Gus's head snapped up from his pillow chest.

'Sally, is that you? I'll be there tonight, we'll tell your dad about us. I know he hides behind the newspaper muttering, "Yanks! Tall, good looking and cocky. Keep your chocolate and silk stockings. Leave my girl alone", but I love you. Mom will love you too. America's a great place. Oh Sal, wait for me.'

Little Willow appeared on his left, it looked like a coat-of-arms quartered by roads: the grey church and tower, the dark thatch of the pub, the cluster of cottages round the green and the red telephone box.

And then, beyond, to the north, a narrow lighted ribbon widened into the runway.

He needed the landing gear. His right arm lay across his chest, a useless limb.

The engine stopped and that comforting sound of life died into silence. He whispered, 'Thanks Mossie. I knew you would get us home.'

Committed now, it would have to be a dead stick approach. No landing wheels. Glide in. He skimmed over the end of the runway, felt the Mosquito bounce, shudder, scrape the surface of the concrete.

His throat was a dry funnel, but he forced out the words, 'We've made it, Jack.'

Gus let his eyelids fall, his thoughts fade away. He could hear the sound of the rescue bells and, on a sigh, his spirit joined his buddy to go home to the streets of New York.

# JORJA'S RESOLUTION

'I have your diary,' said a male voice.

Jorja Philips held the mobile phone at arm's length and counted to ten, then flipped her straight dark hair back over her shoulder and brought the phone back to her ear. This was a new tack to chat up a girl, 'Who am I speaking to and I have not lost my diary.'

'Karl Bennett, spelt with a K. And, I assure you, I do have it.'

Jorja felt her heartbeat quicken. There was so much personal rubbish scribbled in those pages. 'Hold on a second please.' Putting the phone down, she snatched her handbag from the desk drawer. It weighed a ton. Why did she carry so much? She rummaged round make-up, letters, supermarket receipts and two wallets – why two? Half the cards were out of date and useless. Frustrated, she emptied the contents onto the desktop. Her diary wasn't there. She pulled the lining out willing it to appear like magic.

'So ... you have my diary. Where did you find it?'

'In the park; lying under the seat by the rose garden.'

He was so controlled, authoritative and now that the initial panic had eased, she liked the sound of his voice.

'Where did you get my number?'

'From your diary. Where else would I get it?'

'You've been reading my diary! How dare you pry into my ...'

'Hey, I only looked at the detail page. How else was I going to know who to call?' His manner changed. 'I'm not a peeping Tom, if that's what you think.'

'Sorry, it's just ...' Jorja felt so stupid and her cheeks burnt with humiliation. 'Can you post it back to me, please? You have the address.'

'I've a better idea. Have lunch with me. 12.30 in the park.'

He didn't wait for an answer, and it left her no choice if she wanted the diary back.

Jorja sat on the edge of the park seat, head down, feeling more like a honeybee than the stinging wasp on

44

the phone earlier. A pair of long legs filled her view and a voice asked, 'Hello. Are you Jorja Philips?'

She looked up. 'Yes. You're Karl Bennett?' Of course he was. What a dumb thing to say and she bit her lower lip to stop it trembling. Big girls don't cry, but she was so nervous. Was this how a blind date started? Two strangers, eyeing each other up and wondering what they had let themselves in for? What if he was a serial killer, a rapist or a kidnapper? He didn't look evil. In fact, she liked what she saw. Stop, she warned herself, keep it strictly business. Get the diary and go. He sat down beside her. She caught the tang of aftershave on his rugged face and his complexion hinted moors and mountains. Even sitting down she had to tilt her head to look into his green eyes and his hair was the colour of a new thatch.

Jorja smiled and two dimples dented her cheeks.

He raised an eyebrow, 'Am I such a clown?'

'No, of course not. I'm sorry; I didn't mean to be rude.'

'No offence taken. Are you ready for lunch?' He took a brown takeaway bag from behind his back.

Jorja blinked in surprise. This was lunch? Sandwiches sat on a park bench. What had she expected, a three course á la carte at the Ritz? Seated, served, eaten and back to the office within an hour. Wake up girl! This is reality, a hurried snack out of a bag.

'This is kind of you.'

'My pleasure, Jorja. I hope you like chicken and mayonnaise. It's what my sister eats, so I assumed ...'

'Yes, I do.' As she took the cellophane pack from him her fingers brushed his. They were warm, slightly hardened. Yet he wore a dark business suit.

They sat in the shade of a tree, relaxed, no awkwardness between them. He told her he was an architect – not yet famous – but there was time. She guessed he was in his mid-thirties. He didn't mention a wife. He could have a partner. Weddings were going out of fashion in the twenty-first century. She and Paul had been an item. Parting had been civilised. Split the merchandise and wave good-bye. Yet the trauma seemed as hurtful and messy as divorce. Never again for her! She was a free agent. No ties. That had been her New Year's resolution.

'Will you have dinner with me tonight?'

Jorja's brown eyes widened in her oval face and pink lips parted, but no words were spoken. Instead her heart thumped against her ribs and butterflies fluttered in her stomach. 'No ... thank you. I'll just have my diary. It's time to go back to the office.' She sprang off the seat like a jack-in-the-box and held out her hand.

'Hey, I didn't say I wanted you for dinner. Do I look like a cannibal?'

'No, of course you don't. It's just that I'm not into dating ... period.'

'That bad was it? Join the club. Mine left me at the altar.'

Jorja was stunned. She and Paul had skirted round marriage talk, but jilted, that was really sad news. 'I'm sorry to hear that, but the answer is still, no. May I have my diary, please? I'll be late if I don't go now.'

Karl stood and took an oblong black book from his jacket pocket and placed it in her palm. 'See you around, sometime.' He walked away in the direction he had arrived.

Jorja's Saturday began like any other weekend, the luxury of an extra hour in bed and a leisurely breakfast eaten at the table. Then the doorbell rang. The long slender box held twelve pink carnations with a card. She read, *I will pick you up at 12 noon, Karl.* The surprise brought a glow to her cheeks then they reddened with anger. What did he think she was? An easy pickup sweetened by a few flowers? He would get an unanswered door. In fact, she needed groceries, which is where she would be at noon.

She hunted for a car park space. There were queues at every till and negotiating the roundabout, dodging manic drivers, left Jorja sorry she had come. Just to avoid facing Karl Bennett! Cowardice had reaped its reward.

Back at the apartment block she pushed the lift button. At the fourth floor, using her back to prop open the door she slid half a dozen plastic bags into the corridor. The pinging frenzy of the lift mechanism deadened any footsteps and two masculine hands picked up the bags.

Hot and flustered Jorja looked up at Karl Bennett. Cool, fresh and groomed – the exact opposite to her.

'May I carry your bags, ma'am?' He was laughing at her. Not out loud, just that smug-man-thing-versus-silly-woman-thing.

Jorja wanted to say, no thank you, I can manage, but it would make her look more stupid than she already felt. 'I live at number 16 ... oh ... you already know that.'

Inside her kitchen, she asked, 'Would you like a coffee before you leave?' That would put him in his place, she thought. He had managed to manoeuvre his way into her apartment with the bags, but he needn't think it was an invite for the night.

'I'm not an ogre, Jorja. The flowers were a gift, nothing else. Why did you leave me knocking at an empty apartment?'

There was something in his voice that made her look at him.

'How do you see me – friend or foe?'

Jorja needed to be honest. This man had faced one let-down, he didn't deserve another. 'I'm sorry about today, but I'm not ready to get cosy ... with anyone.'

'I'll take a rain check on the coffee. Put your shopping away. I'll let myself out.'

The door latch clicked closed.

Jorja sighed and two teardrops splashed onto a plastic bag.

The desk was a shambles.

Jorja flung files aside to reach the phone.

'Graphics Design, Jorja Philips speaking.'

'You're very efficient, Miss Philips. You make me hesitant to ask you out for a park lunch?'

'Karl … persistent Bennett suits you. OK, chicken sandwich and a Coke. See you at 12.30, must go.' She dropped the handset back and smiled, two could play at no choices.

In the park Jorja sat waiting for Karl, pretending to read a magazine. When he arrived he stopped a few feet from the bench and she looked up and gave him a welcoming smile.

'That's a start to a friendship, Brown Eyes. I love your smile.'

Their park bench lunches became regular dates over the next few weeks.

Karl tried several times to ask Jorja out at the weekend, but she held firm to her resolution. One Friday, as they parted, he said, 'I'm away on a business trip to Holland next week. I'll be in touch. See you.' He was gone before she could say goodbye.

Her weekend started as normal, but as Saturday slid into Sunday, Jorja became reluctant to face Monday, knowing that if she went to the park for lunch, she would sit alone. Why had she let herself look forward to Karl's company? Become involved, laughing at his jokes, listening to stories about his work and walks across the downs. How foolish she had been to refuse his invitations.

Seven lonely days dragged by.

On the Monday, Jorja waited for Karl's call. It didn't come.

Each day when the phone rang, she pounced on it like a cat after a mouse, but it seemed Karl had become the invisible man. On Friday, just before leaving, she picked up the phone and dialled his office and was told he was not available. Well, it was the brush off she deserved, but it didn't stop her heart breaking in two.

She lay awake that night watching the clock tick past two, three, four o'clock. As the dawn chorus chirped the sun above the horizon, Jorja let the tears fall, as they never had when she and Paul had parted.

Saturday shoppers bustled round Jorja with enthusiasm. They seemed to be the happiest people alive, compared to her misery that deepened by the hour. Karl had accepted her rejection. Saw no future with a woman as indecisive as his last? The business trip had allowed him to end what was a fruitless affair for him. But she was as much to blame because she hadn't explained why. Did he think she was playing with him like a puppet on a string?

When she reached her block of flats the lift had a hand written notice taped to the door. OUT OF ORDER. She put the bags down. 'That's all I need. Why did I buy all those tin vegetables? I hate them anyway. Now I've got to lug them up four flights of stairs.'

Her morning was going from bad to worse. Her mind was a muddle of thoughts, her arms feeling like they were being pulled out of their sockets when she finally dumped the grocery bags onto her corridor floor.

Two tanned hands picked them up. 'Carry your bags, ma'am?'

Jorja jerked up and burst into tears, blubbering, 'I thought you didn't want me,' and threw herself at him.

The bags slid from Karl's fingers and he hugged her close. 'At last! I've waited weeks for you to thaw, Ice Lady. You're the only person I know that has kept a New Year's resolution going for more than a few days. I'll see you don't make any more this side of the next twenty years.'

'Is that a proposal, Karl Bennett?'

'Shall we call it half a proposal, Miss Jorja Philips? We need to spend much more time together before we make it a whole. We'll start with going out to dinner this evening.'

Jorja pulled away from him. 'Hey! How do you know about my 'Anti-Man' campaign?'

'I couldn't resist a quick peep at your January 1st page.'

'Karl Bennett ... you ...' Brushing away the tears, she smiled. 'I need to make one more entry,' and she snuggled into him again. 'Diary lost and love found in the park.'

# THE DIARIES

The wind blew pages of the diary like washing on a line.

Strengthening, from the east, a pale yellow light crept into the sky and the early morning breeze lessened. White pages lay open and flicked over, one by one.

**Monday**

The queue was endless. Everyone knew that the sausages were 'off the ration' today. There's never enough for all, but I got mine. I've run out of points this month, so everything will have to be without sugar. Thank goodness Mike and Margery get their milk at school. The weather is still very cold and we've run out of coal. I feel like a wound-up spring; this stretching out the food, make do and mend, hand-me downs. God, how did we get to this? Maybe the news will be better tomorrow.

**The queue was endless, everyone stocking up for the forthcoming siege. The shelves are now empty. Coming home, my car held such a small amount of shopping: tins, dry-food packets and candles, torches and batteries. All the chocolate was gone. Masud and Shireen will not be pleased. Allah, how did we get to this? Maybe the news will be better tomorrow.**

**Tuesday**

The factory was hectic today. We were down on our quota, because my machine broke down – again! I couldn't stay on. Mum's on the late shift at the Odeon, so I needed to get home to the little ones. Aunt Gwen usually helps out, but she's now working on the trolleys as a clippie. I heard today that Cousin Joan has gone to the country to do farm work. I'm so tired; perhaps the news will be better tomorrow.

**Ahmed went to work. Masud and Shireen to school. I've stacked the supplies and sorted out the essential clothing. Everywhere there is fear. Who can we trust? No one. Not even our friends or colleagues. The TV is still alive, but the**

outlook is not good. I'm so tired; perhaps the news will be better tomorrow.

## Wednesday

We've been living each night in the shelter, now in the daytime too. I cradle my two children, thankful that they cannot hear the drone of a V1 or the sudden silence as it falls to earth. Why, oh why, must men wage war and leave the women to weep. How I hate this enemy without.

**The sandbags are in place; we are barricaded in our home. I cradle my two children, thankful that they cannot hear the whine of a Cruise Missile or know when it falls to earth. Why, oh why, do I not have the freedom of speech? How I hate this enemy within.**

The Rescue worker dug in the rubble.

He picked up a diary. Brushing off the dust he stopped to read. It was a woman's. A dark dried blood stain obscured the date – 1944 or 2003? The same result, only a lifetime in between.

# TURNING OF THE SEASON

The fourth season is upon us and my thin blanket does not keep out the cold night air. I cannot sleep for my mind is too troubled. Like any other morning, I can hear the scratching of the rats, big fat rats that eat the rotting scraps in the streets. My four babes may come to that if Husband does not soon find work.

I wait and watch for the dawn light to show from the hole in the ceiling, our way out by ladder to the Pawnbrokers shop floor. We live here, four families, in this cellar room with its hard earth floor and damp brick walls. There is a fireplace, but it is used only when there is something to cook. If I look up into the flue, I can feel a whisper of fresh air coming down the chimney on to my face. The same cannot be said of this cellar, the air smells of dirty bodies and stinking buckets.

What madness brought us to a place like this? Fools we were to listen to that stranger's words, that there was 'much money to be earned in the great town of Manchester'. It made Husband yearn to come. Perhaps, if we had come last year, when there were fewer people, we would not be in this dark hole now.

Husband is getting up. His bones will be aching as much as mine, lying as we are, on a bed of rags. There is little to be gained if I get up, I have only tainted water to offer him – it is from the ditch that has the likes of our bucket in it; dead fish and sodden vegetables floating on top. We all use it; take turns to get the jug filled.

Maybe today he will be pointed at by the factory manager – you are in – perhaps today he will be lucky. There's movement from the other men. Are their wives thinking the same as me? I'm a mother who loves her children, yet, when they wake, I must watch them cry for food I do not have.

The ladder is creaking with four pairs of feet. Like brothers in war, they move forth to win the battle to work. There is no fear of death by the sword, but of their starving families. If Husband returns again, unwanted, I have one thing left to sell to our landlord – my wedding ring. He will not wait for his rent when there are so many other country folk flooding in looking for their pot of gold. I wish I could warn them of the despair they will come to know. Tell them how we were hoodwinked with promises and cunning words. I want them to return to their homes and be thankful they have neighbours and friends to help when life gets hard. Here, in this town of thousands, no one has a thought for us, not even those who sleep near me now. It's only their selves they think of – survive or die. I must move. My aches are so great.

I am the first to rise. I know the others are awake; there is no snuffling or snores. This living together is so strange for me. I try to keep us private, but there are twenty to share one table and four stools. These are kept for the men. We have no cupboards; just a shelf and what pots and plates we each brought are shared. My beautiful copper pot is now black; it was my mother's wedding present, my dearest possession.

My days are just bearable. I take the children into the streets and beg for scraps from the barrow-boys. Those who have made their fortunes throw pennies like raindrops and I scramble with the other women for my share. But the nights are pitiful as Husband and I try to comfort each other, for all to hear.

I can walk from this place: leave behind the towering factories; alleyways filled with beggars who go to sleep and never wake up, and cellars filled with disillusioned souls like us, living with the constant filth and hunger.

I can go back to the country where berries grow, carrots and turnips fill our stomachs and cows give milk. Run in the woods, collect branches and light a fire; find a barn to bed my babes in fresh straw. Walk to the hamlet of cottages where I know there will be a welcome for us. I need not take much, I can carry the babe on my back, the little one in my arms and the other two can walk. Oh! The urge is so great, I can't think of anything else. Even my hungry stomach has stopped hurting. I can drink from the stream, clear and sweet, as it flows over the pebbles. I can go now – wake them and go.

I can hear the sound of feet on the ladder, one, two, three pairs of feet. Who has been the lucky one today? I hold my breath – if the lucky man is not Husband, I must go, to save my little ones. The first man has a lighted candle and it is not Husband. My heart is pounding so hard it is almost a pain. Behind him the second man is not Husband. Please, please, let the last not be him. Hurry, I want to see who you are – glory, it is a stranger stepping from the last rung. Hope, merciful hope is mine - thanks be to God – he is a chosen one today. We will eat tonight and I will stay, as is my place, beside Husband.

The four pennies I have sewn into the hem of my dress I can keep for another day.

# ASK THE GREMLINS

'Have you seen my keys?'

'No.'

'They were here yesterday.'

'Which keys?'

'Door keys.'

'No.'

'I've looked everywhere. Are you sure?'

'Yes.'

'Have a look for me.'

'No.'

'Why not? I'm late, can I have yours?'

'No.'

'Will you be here when I get back?'

'No.'


Drawers open and shut. Cupboard doors bang.

It's a repeat performance every time.

Wait for it – here it comes – another set of keys to be cut?

'Lend me yours, I'll pop down the shop to get a new set.'

'Another fiver less for the savings fund.'

'Look on the bright side, a spare set when we find them.'


Three months later.

'Pass my Wellingtons. Best take them on holiday; then it won't rain.'

'What's that rattling inside the right boot?'

'A set of door keys.'

'How did they get there?'

'I don't know. Ask the gremlins.'

# REVENGE

Scar Face had killed her baby.

Aerona lay in a hillside cave, her heart filled with hate. She should move, but the pain hurt so much where the enemy's arrow-head was buried deep above her milk-breast. Her breathing changed and became short and sharp, the arrow must be pulled. Even strong fighting men became weak from such wounds; she must defy that weakness. Her lips moved in a silent chant, her prayer to the Anger God, calling to him to fill her with strength. He must answer her plea, revenge must be hers: a life for a life, her slaughtered baby for Scar Face's baby.

She began to shiver as the cold night air filled the cave. Without light she was like a blind woman. Without warmth certain death awaited her. She needed fire to sear her flesh and stop the bleeding. Aerona knelt, and even though she hugged her elbow into her body the pain intensified beyond endurance. Sweeping her free hand in an arc she searched for anything that would burn. With an animal's instinct her fingers found dry boughs and she stripped the bark into a heap. Getting a flame proved difficult as she struggled to rub two boughs together between her fingers; then she smelt smoke. It rose like a scent and she blew gently until a flame ate into the bark. Aerona chanted a prayer of thanks as she added her hoard of wood.

Warmth spread through her. Now was the time. There would be but a moment of lucidity after she touched her skin, then her mind would close to the cave around her. Aerona gripped the broken shaft, breathed deeply and pulled. Terror raced through her as the skin ripped and the arrow-head burst forth. She threw it away and picked up a glowing bough and held it against the wound. The smell of burning flesh filled her nostrils and her vision wavered, she needed another moment. Enough! She threw the torture weapon into the fire and fell backwards into oblivion.

Aerona opened her eyes. Darkness had turned into morning light. Pain raced through her left shoulder, breast and ribs. She touched the charred wound and felt no bleeding, but she was weak and thirsty. With great effort, she knelt and crawled to the cave entrance.

Her village was in ruins.

The land had been ravished. Why had the hill warriors come to her village with such murderous intent? There was plenty for all – they were blessed with forests, beasts for meat; rivers full of fish. What had her people done to deserve this massacre?

But there were survivors – men, women and children were coming out of the forest and across the river. She could not see Elphin among them. The last time she had seen him he had been defending her and Mabon. Amidst the cries of battle, and the smoke from their burning homes, Elphin had shouted at her to run for the woods. Then out of the mayhem, Scar Face had roared his war cry and aimed his arrow. When she had opened her eyes Mabon lay slain beside her. She had cradled him, cried out her anguish and ran to hide.

She picked up her cold, still son. Her breasts were full of milk, but he would never feed again. What she needed now was time to heal. Then revenge would be hers.


Two full moons passed its cycle.

Aerona knelt in the cave. She chanted words of thanks for her life, words of sorrow for her husband who she had found slain in the village. She chanted words of heartache for her baby son. When she placed the death stones upon their graves her vengeance had soared. Her only regret was that her own grave would be far from them, maybe not a grave at all. She did not expect to be given such a right by her enemy.

She had chosen to wear a wolf skin tunic in preference to her usual cloth dress and had tied her dark hair high with a braided deer sinew. Everything she needed for the journey was in a goat skin bag. She bowed her head, rose from the dirt and left.

Aerona ran up the sloping grassland; pass the shepherd boy and his grazing sheep to a path that led her into the mountains.

When the sun reached its zenith she slowed her pace. The track became steeper, but she didn't stop; the power of her revenge driving her on. Her mind focused on the hill fort village of her enemy. She climbed onwards over hillocks of poor grassland and scrub; slithered down gullies of loose shifting stones until the sun slipped into its dark bed.

Aerona crawled under a thorn bush to protect her from the night animals. She was very tired; hill walking was not a way of life for the River People. The water she carried quenched her thirst and the dried deer meat filled her stomach. The night breeze died away and the leaves on the bush stilled. She could now hear every sound: the scratching of claws, the baying of a wolf, the snuffles of small creatures and something ran across her shoulder. She lay down and clasped her hands around her knees. She was not frightened, yet feared what was out there. The sounds of the night gradually ceased and beyond her prickly haven she sensed something magical cloaking the high peaks as their jagged teeth disappeared into the dark heaven of the after world. Was one of the tiny sparkling dots Mahon? Was another, a little larger, her Elphin? When she had taken her revenge, would the After World God allow her into his kingdom? The thought troubled her as she fell asleep.

Sunlight and blue sky greeted her when she woke. The path she found was well marked and she set a good pace. By the zenith, Aerona reached the top of a rocky rise and judged she could make the Hill People's settlement before dark. She ate the last of her food and saved half the water. Thirst was her biggest danger as she travelled the unknown land. She pushed on and followed a much used track. As the day neared its end, the fort came into view.

At the stony fire-break she stopped. She thought over her plan to find Scar Face. He was large of height and body. On his tunic he had worn the badge of a leader – the wolf. Her only knowledge was what she had heard from her own tribal elders – their enemies fighting strength, their fierceness, and how their homes were bigger and stronger than the River People's huts. She took a cloth cloak from her bag and wrapped it round her shoulders, pulled the hood low over her forehead.

Two guards knocked the wedges from the gate as Aerona walked boldly forward, her height and stature small in contrast to the guards, but she was not challenged. Inside, the pathways were deserted. Home and traders dwellings looked the same – only those with their trestles outside showed the difference.

Aerona felt conspicuous. Perhaps she should have waited until the morning when the roads would be busy, but her smallness would still bring attention. At least she could move swiftly in the shadows. Listening at a door she heard voices and a baby crying. This must be the home of a worker or fighting man. She didn't waste time on the other huts and at the end of the path came into a deserted circular space. Four roads led from it, like the lines on her stone dress brooch that Elphin had given her as a symbol of commitment on the day the Chief Elder blessed them in marriage. But, which road would lead her to Scar Face? If she had to search each one the night would be over and she could be captured and enslaved. The raiders had taken many maidens from her village, virgins too young to be committed. She had heard stories that they were used as play things for the young fighters who awaited their first battle.

Without warning, music and singing came from the opposite road, lighted torches flared and people spilled into the circular arena. Aerona cringed back against a wall. This was all wrong, she had not come to witness merriment; her heart was too full of destruction. She was here to kill Scar Face and his son. The space filled and she stepped forward into the fringe of the crowd.

Behind her a voice asked. 'Are you on your own, little one?' A young fighter – wearing a cloak of sewn fox skins, held in place with its claws signalled his lowly rank.

He thought her a girl?

'Yes. I am on an errand for my mistress.'

'Cannot she wait a while? Come, the dancing is starting.'

He took her hand and pulled her into the circle and they joined the other dancers. This would be her undoing. She was the only small person in the whole circle. The young fighter pulled her hood back revealing her dark untidy hair. She should have taken time to assemble her appearance, but she was here only to fulfil one purpose – her revenge as executioner.

'You are a beautiful maiden,' he touched her cheek, 'we shall dance until the dawn.'

'Sire, I have my duties to perform, it is impossible.'

'Then, just this one dance and I will deem my passion spent.'

The melodic music felt like a caress as the dancers dipped and swayed. Aerona knew nothing of their rituals but the dance was sensual and she copied the movements of the woman beside her. The young fighter drew her towards him, his eyes reflecting the torchlight. He claimed her by the waist and slipped the loop free from her brooch and her cloak fell over his arm.

'What a strange creature you are. You are not from this fort?'

'I did not say. I am a servant and have no choice but to follow my mistress.'

He guided her away into the shadow of a building and the sound of the music faded. The fighter took a handful of her loose hair below the sinew, pulled her head back.

'Who is your master?' His voice no longer held the cajoling purr of a feline.

Aerona had no answer, her name for him was Scar Face, yet she must answer the fighter's question.

'He is a Head Man. I am a lowly servant and know him only by his appearance – Scar Face.'

The fighter's handsome features changed from seducer to interrogator.

'Disrespect is not something we tolerate. He was our greatest warrior, and led our people in many great battles. His last journey was beyond the many hills and valleys to the River People. He was slain and is now with our war lord that roams the night sky.'

The fighter looked over his shoulder and signalled to someone in the crowd. 'Why do you not know of this?'

He had become suspicious. What excuse could she give? She would not let him stop her mission. After, it did not matter if she died, she would be with Elphin and her son.

'His death is so new. I still think of him here.'

'Two full moons have passed. Tell me, what is the name of your mistress?'

Aerona drew the knife from her belt. Looking into his eyes she smiled and stepped closer. With her free hand she touched his cheek and raised herself on to her toes. 'Let me tell you my story, young fighter, as my lips touch yours.'

He pulled her close. 'Come, we will go into the shadow a little more, my strange servant girl.'

He was so sure of his charm. Aerona enticed him with a soft inviting kiss on his lips and whispered, 'You will be my first fighter, sire.'

He drew her into the darkness of a porch. She moved close, raised her head and claimed his lips. Her knife plunged into his heart. The fighter's hold on her tightened, his cry trapped by her kiss. His eyes widened with shock and disbelief and then they closed.

Aerona let him fall back against the door. There was no regret in her heart; he was the enemy. She wiped her knife on his cloak and replaced it into its sheath. A moment of triumph ran through her: a life for a life – Elphin's life.

She had to find the Wolf Leader's home. She moved in the shadows round the arena, taking the road the people had come from. There was little difference until she reached a cross section. The change told her she had made the correct choice. Out of the night larger dwellings emerged – dark and formidable.

The music stopped and a rabble of voices rose from behind her. They had found the fighter.

Which abode? They were all similar and she could see no distinguishing badges or colours; no sounds came from either side as she ran along the path. Breathless she reached a corner. One lighted hut stood out in the darkness.

Into the night a woman's cry of agony filled the air. What monstrous happenings were being performed inside? She reached the door and heard another cry. The same cry she had made months ago – a birth cry.

Leaning her head on the door she felt weak. Who was behind this door? She searched for some identification and her fingers traced a raised block, she needed light to see, the moon was not strong enough. The neighbouring hut had a lighted torch in a sheath and she hurried to take it. The block had the symbol of a wolf.

Aerona sank to her knees and lifted her head to the sky and cried out, 'Praise to thee my Anger God for your guidance. My revenge is nigh.'

The flickering torchlight of the villagers was coming closer; she had but a few minutes. After her revenge it would not matter, they could kill her.

The cries of Scar Face's woman increased to a crescendo of absolute surrender. The following silence hurt as much as her cries. It was over, she had delivered her child.

Aerona drew her knife. Revenge was now hers.

The dimly lit room was a scene of horror. The woman was alone; her child between her legs, still and lifeless – the Anger God had taken his own revenge.

The woman looked at her, tears falling from her eyes – a waterfall of grief that Aerona understood. She should kill the woman, now! Send her to the after world with her baby. She had the right to her revenge and stepped forward, raised her blade, all she had to do was plunge it into Scar Face's woman's heart. Her hand stilled; the weeks of hatred drained from her.

The face looking at her was old, the hair grey, she was almost beyond child bearing time.

'Please, no,' the woman's words were hoarse, 'water, please.'

Aerona wavered, she didn't know what to do – a pitcher was on a table. Without thought of good or evil, she half-filled a cup and went to the woman, lifted her head so she could drink.

'Where is your birth nurse?' Aerona was angry, not with vengeance, but pity.

'It came so quick. Help me. I know my child is dead.'

Aerona stared at the mother. She was the enemy. Her husband had killed. Like she had now killed. The people were coming for her. But she was also a mother. A kinswoman regardless of what tribe they held their allegiance to.

'All right. I must burn my knife.'

The candle flame licked both sides of the blade as Aerona slid it through.

She worked quickly, blocking out the shouts of fury from the approaching crowd.

'Please, give me my child. I must hold him just once.'

Aerona took the cloth she held and covered the baby, lifted it gently. A grief so strong spread through her, her own pain bonding with an enemy she should hate. She placed the bundle into the woman's arms.

'Go. I will not tell.'

Aerona hesitated. A chance of life or confront her enemy?

There was no choice.

She walked out of the door and on into the after world.

# BAND OF GOLD

First the gift of the diamond ring.

'Oh! How wonderful, you're engaged,' chorus the girlie friends.

'Well, you're on your way now. Just the little band of gold to come,' coos mother.

They spend days shopping for the perfect gown. Wedding presents arriving day by day. Enough towels to last a lifetime and a Chinese vase that will never see the light of day. But lots of useful dishes, pots and pans; some folks remembered their list.

The Day arrives. He slips the band of gold onto her finger, his gift of love.

Year one is the paper anniversary.

She got baby congratulation cards. He got a cigar.

Year two is cotton.

Hubby was being cautious, bought a high-neck nightie.

Come year three, its leather.

Money's a bit short. A pair of new shoes would be nice.

Year four is fruit or flowers.

They doubled as an offering as he walked for the second time down the Maternity Ward.

Year five is wood.

The new garden shed was a place for him to hide.

Six, seven, eight and nine.

Passed in a flash with Beaver Cubs' and Brownies' camps.

Year ten is tin.

The chicken coop fell down. Frozen birds filled the freezer for months.

Eleven is steel.

This was a black time. The factory closed down.

Sexy twelve and thirteen quotes silk and lace.

Forget that! Teenage tantrums took their place.

Fourteen is ivory.

He searched until...A trio of elephants sits on the windowsill.

Fifteen years.

A beautiful crystal necklace. Where did the money come from?

Twenty years is china.

What can he come up with for that – maybe a porcelain spaniel – not this year.

Her precious has tickets for two, so they can walk hand-in-hand along the Great China Wall.

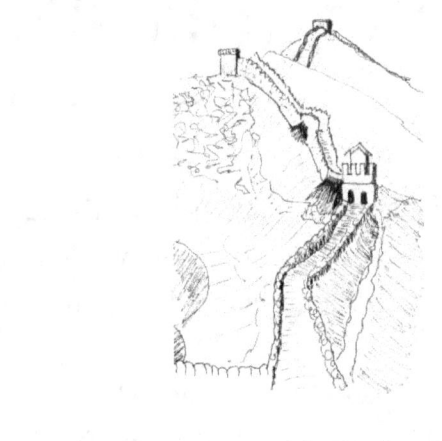

# SUNLIGHT TRAINING

Wilf shuffled for a space in the coal miner's lift.

This was his last ride up. Never again would he taste the coal dust or joke with his mates deep in the bowels of the earth.

The government had won. He was redundant – too old to retrain. But how long would the pay-off last? How long before he'd have to ask for social benefits? Could he face that? No. He would sooner jump back down the shaft than face that humiliation.

When Wilf reached his two-up, two-down mid-terrace house, he stood outside, reluctant to go in. Shame stood alongside his anger. He'd been bottling up his feelings for the past two weeks, since he'd opened the letter passed to him by the pit manager.

The house was empty; it always was when he was on the early shift. God, how was he going to face the pitying glances from the other men's wives? He put the key in the lock and went in. He would go straight to bed, then there was no chance of seeing anyone until tomorrow. It would give him a few hours to adjust. Adjust! Who was he kidding?

Wilf didn't sleep. He lay there thinking about the pit and about money and listening to the tick of the alarm clock. At last the shrill ring sounded, he'd been in bed twelve hours. It was time to get up. But it wasn't necessary and it wouldn't be now until the day he died.

The sound of footsteps on the stairs told him his daughter, Molly, was going to make the tea. She also knew there was no reason to get up so early now, it was just habit.

'And neither can I,' he muttered, 'not another minute.' He pushed back the covers. It was a luxury he had never known and he didn't intend to start now. His feet touched the rag rug and he stood up and turned on the light. What was he going to wear? Not his miner's clothes. He opened the wardrobe door – there was his dark suit for funerals, his sports jacket and grey trousers he wore when he went to the Tattersley Miners' Club. It would have to be the greys. He opened the chest of drawers and took out a white shirt, socks, vest and pants and laid them on the bed.

When his Hilda died, Molly, who had recently been widowed, gave up her rented house and moved in with him. The only awkward thing about it was that he had always washed downstairs. Standing half-dressed at the scullery sink, with Molly around, was a tad embarrassing. So he'd decided to get a plumber to put a wash basin in his room and then life carried on much the same.

Now he filled that basin with hot water, lathered his face and shaved. Washed his face and neck and dried with a coarse towel. He took his false teeth from a glass of diluted bleach and rinsed them with cold water.

It was strange slipping his arms into a cotton shirt, instead of the dark flannel. He tucked the tails inside his trousers and buttoned the fly; then picked up a shoehorn to help his feet into his best shoes. He always polished them to a brilliant shine after every outing, so at least he had one job to do every day.

As he passed the mirror on the wardrobe door it reflected a sight never allowed in the bedroom - his dull black work boots. He felt choked, almost bereaved, for his life now gone. He wiped his eyes with his knuckles.

It was time to go and face Molly.

'Good morning, Dad. We're a pair of dafties, getting up at this hour. We could both have had a lay-in. Still, I've made the tea. Sit down.'

Wilf sat in his usual chair, but he felt uncomfortable. What could he say to Molly? They usually only grunted at each other – he would have drunk his tea, picked up his sandwiches and left.

'Thanks.' He looked round the room. It hadn't changed much since he'd carried Hilda over the threshold forty years ago. This was where they lived – he called it the kitchen, Molly called it the living room. There was the mahogany table and four chairs, sideboard and two stuffed green armchairs. The only additions to mark the twentieth century, was a stereo radio and a colour telly. He had felt that Molly deserved some modern pleasures when she moved in.

'Do you want any breakfast, Dad?'

Wilf looked at her and smiled, 'Why not? I've plenty of time now.'

'Bacon and egg?'

'It's not Sunday, Molly. I don't know. What are you going to have?'

'Oh, I just have toast and Marmite.'

'Then, I'll have the same.'

Molly went out into the scullery and Wilf heard her strike a match and then the rattle of the enamel grill tray.

It was only five o'clock. What was he going to do all day?

Molly called, 'Dad, if you have time, there's a bit of veg left in the shed, can you get it, I want to make a stew.'

Wilf didn't answer.

'Dad, did you hear me?'

'Yes. I suppose so. When do you want them?'

'By half-past seven, please. They have to simmer for several hours so we can have dinner at one o'clock.'

This was a new world for Wilf. Doing shift work had meant he ate either before or after a shift. Now he could have three meals a day sitting with Molly. What were they going to talk about? She didn't want to hear about the coal face or smirking men laughing at tales that weren't fit for women's ears.

'Right then, I'll do it straight after the toast.'

Molly came back and put two plates on the table and sat down.

'Gwen at the corner shop is on holiday this week. I said I would help out. I have to be there at eight. Will you be all right?'

Wilf felt like a small boy. How had he gone from a miner, who risked life and limb year after year, to a dependent who couldn't be left for a few hours?

'I think, Molly, I can manage not to fall over or hurt myself. I've been doing it ever since I went to work nearly fifty years ago. Don't start fussing now.'

Molly sighed. 'Sorry, Dad, but ... well, this is all new to you ... I mean, having nothing to do.'

Nothing to do!

Wilf let these three words roll round in his mind. They horrified him. 'I'll go and get the veg. You get yourself ready. I'll be fine.'

The sun was over the housetops that backed on to his row. Normally, he would only have had this fresh air walking to the pithead. He breathed in. The air felt cold slipping down his throat, stinging with pinpoint jabs. He closed his lips tight, then opened and breathed in again. This time he knew what to expect and enjoyed the sensation. He did it several times more. He would remember this as the first new experience of his retirement.

'Dad, can I have the veg, time's getting on.'

Wilf waved, 'Coming.'

After Molly left the house it was very quiet.

Sitting in his chair, the one to the left of the fireplace, he pondered whether to turn on the telly. Morning programmes were for the women or schools. But what else was there to do? Hilda had kept house and he'd earned the money. It was as it should be, as had his father and his before him.

Wilf turned the television on and a news reader filled the screen. He tuned to another channel – an advert for grass fertiliser, demanding that the viewer tend their gardens with weekly nourishment. The screen flicked to Stork margarine – two young women trying to tell the difference from butter. He turned it off.

They didn't have much grass, just a small patch to sit on in the back. It always looked weedy and those wretched daisies and clover made up most of it anyway. Perhaps, as he had time now he could make an effort to give Molly something nice to sit on. Do a few flowers in a border. He had always grown veg – Hilda had insisted; said they tasted better than those from Greenfingers in the High Street.

After a cup of chicory-flavoured coffee, Wilf thought about the grass again. It would be a token of his appreciation, Molly never asked him to do much, just the jobs she couldn't manage. Ten minutes later, Wilf locked the front door and set off for the local garden nursery. He reckoned it was about a two mile walk – another first for him – his usual distance was the half-mile to the club for a pint or the same to the pit.

He was out of breath by the time he arrived at Snelgrove Nurseries. It was surrounded by a privet hedge with a wooden gate anchored open. In the centre was an oversized shed with a sign saying: Everything you want for your garden – Come on in. That sounded like a good invitation, so he did just that.

'Good morning, sir. If there's anything you can't see, just ask. I'm Charlie.'

Wilf looked at the shelves – bottles and cans stood like soldiers in rows. Watering cans, netting and plant pots covered the floor, leaving barely enough room for him to walk round.

'I'm looking for grass fertiliser,' said Wilf, twisting his neck to try and locate what he wanted.

'It's third shelf on the left behind you.'

'Thanks.'

'Are you new to the area?'

Wilf wanted to laugh at that. 'No. I've lived all my life in Tattersley.'

'Just retired, then?'

'Well ... yes, I suppose I am.'

Wilf's life crowded in on him. No, he wasn't retired, he was unwanted. There were years left in him to work the pit, but they'd said no. Be a good man and take the money – sit back and enjoy retirement. He didn't want retirement – he wanted to work.

Suddenly the shop seemed to shrink and close in on him. 'I'll just go and have a look outside – be back in a minute.'

Wilf wasn't really interested; it was just an excuse to get away from the man. But as he walked, he noticed the shrubs and plants along the paths. They added colour amongst the green leaves – new life struggling to grow – waiting for those keen gardeners to pluck them from the trays and set them into the earth; waiting for gentle rain and warm sun to make them blossom. These thoughts chased away Wilf's dark moment and he wandered amongst the foliage enjoying it far more than he would have ever thought.

After much deliberation, Wilf took a tray each of polyanthus and pansies, four rose bushes – one of each colour – back into the shop.

'That's a good start for the season, sir. Did you want the grass feed?'

'Yes, please.'

The man came round from the counter. He limped, much the same as Wilf did when his knee ached.

'A touch of arthritis, I'm afraid. Standing a lot plays it up.'

'That makes two of us. Got mine down the black hole.'

'This isn't a large nursery to run, but I think Old Father Time is trying to tell me something. I've run this place for ten years single-handed, since my Doris passed away, but I think now's the time to seek a little help.'

Wilf nodded, understanding that both of them were suffering, but in different ways.

'I didn't want to give up either. The pit was my world, my life, like gardening is yours. Ageing can be a bum of a cross to bear. This is my first day of retirement. They think they are doing me a favour, but they're not. I want to work.'

The man nodded. 'A bum cross to bear,' and tapped in the prices of Wilf's goods.

'Will you be paying by cheque or cash?'

'Cash. Is taking cheques a good idea?'

'It's the latest thing now. The white collar workers are all being paid that way.'

'Oh.' There didn't seem anything else to say.

Wilf parted with his money and realised he wasn't going to be able to carry it all home.

'Stupid me, I can't carry that lot two miles. I'll have to come back this afternoon for some of it.'

'You don't have a car then?'

'No. Never had a use for one – shift work doesn't lend itself to gallivanting about.'

'Sorry, I don't deliver. Although ... what if I come after closing time?'

'It would be a help. Sure you don't mind?'

'Take what you want for today and I'll see you later with the rest.'

Wilf showed his gratitude with a smile. 'I live at 46 Wheelers Terrace, half way along on the left.' He picked up the box of grass fertilizer, tucked it under his arm and waved goodbye.

\*

At six o'clock, Wilf heard a knock on the front door.

The garden man stood with the tray of pansies in his hand. 'As promised, all goods delivered as ordered.'

'Come in. We'll take them straight through to the back.'

Molly was filling the kettle when both men came into the scullery. 'What's all this about, Dad?'

'This is Charlie, from the garden nursery. He's delivered the goods I bought this morning. It's for a little gardening job I have in mind. Charlie, this is my daughter, Molly.'

'Nice to meet you, Molly.'

'And you, Charlie. This is kind of you.'

'Cuppa when we've finished?'

'Five minutes, Dad, and it'll be ready.'

Wilf put the rose bushes down by the shed. 'Here will do for now. Thanks for bringing them.'

'Glad to help.'

Wilf held his arm out, indicating the wooden bench. 'It's still pleasant, shall we have our tea here. I'm Wilf by the way.'

They sat quietly, looking at the garden.

'A fair size plot,' Charlie commented. 'I see you grow your own veg, and this is a pleasant bit of grass to rest your feet on. South facing too, but not enough to keep you busy all day.'

'No.'

The man's remark dug deep, emphasising the grudge that lodged like a stone in his belly.

'I've been thinking this afternoon about my business. If I had someone to help out, I could advertise a delivery service. What would you say to a part-time job?'

Wilf didn't answer.

'Sorry, I shouldn't have jumped in like a bull in a china shop.'

'No. You just took me by surprise; a part-time job? But I'm no expert on gardening. True, I have always turned my hand to this bit, but help with your lot ...'

'What you do here is no different, not really, mine's just bigger. Whether you grow one carrot or a hundred, the way you do it is the same. I could give you some training. Especially on the bits you might be dodgy with.'

Wilf couldn't think clearly. 'I don't know. Training you say? Like, teaching me the ropes?'

'Yes, and at the going rate per hour.'

'I don't want a charity handout.' Wilf's voice had a bitter note to it.

The man ran his fingers through his sparse grey hair. 'Look, Wilf, there's no charity here; a good day's work for a fair day's pay. You help me and I can help you.'

Wilf sat quietly and thought for a moment about the man's offer. He had worked hard in the darkness of the pit to earn his bread. This was a chance to work in the sunlight to keep that bread on the table. He could breathe in the fresh air each day, as he had this morning. Cleanse his lungs of the black dust. He would be out of Molly's way; give the house to her like she was used to. He could look his mates in the eye when he went to the club for a drink. Buy his round, as he always had.

He was worth training?

Wilf smiled, thinking of that upstart in the pit office.

Straightening up, he squared his shoulders. 'I'll give it a go, Charlie. Thanks for the offer.'

Charlie held out his hand. 'Done. See you tomorrow at nine o'clock'

As promised, Molly came through the kitchen door carrying a tray. 'Tea's up, boys.'

'Oh, I think we can do better than that,' laughed Wilf. 'Bring out that whisky left from Christmas. I've got a new job to celebrate. Charlie's going to train me up to be a garden salesman!'

Welcome to Snelgrove Nursery

# THE PROMISE

Stacey heard her mother call from the hall. 'Is everyone ready?'

With her two brothers, three pairs of stamping feet hurtled down the stairs, out of the front door and into the car.

Traffic built up as her father turned off the main road and drove along a narrow lane leading to Popstone Airfield where the annual August Bank Holiday air show was blessed with a clear blue sky, light breeze and a large gathering of privately owned aircraft.

Stacey was the most enthusiastic. Her hazel eyes darted from one aircraft to another. 'Look, Dad, a Piper Cub, a Cherokee and a Tiger Moth. Oh, hurry up and park, just there by the rope barrier. That's the best spot.'

Doug Thompson laughed and said, 'Hilary, I think we have a pilot in the making. That space will do fine.'

'I think it's stupid for a girl to fly; only boys have the brains for it,' Michael the eldest piped up.

'I agree. Girls should keep to dollies and cleaning house.' Middle son, John, waggled his fingers from his temple and poked his tongue out at Stacey.

Stacey turned from the window and glared at her brothers. 'You're mean, jealous pigs. I want to do more with my time than watch TV and play computer games. Mum says, "The world is our oyster". We can do anything we like if we put our minds to it.'

'Rubbish, women can't lift bricks, work cranes, can't ...'

'Yes, we can,' Stacey shouted.

'Enough!' The command left Hilary's lips like a drill sergeant, 'Out of the car, all of you. Michael, John, you get the chairs from the boot; Stacey, the picnic basket. Doug, we'll get the ice creams.'

Yes, ma'am, at once.' Doug smiled. 'I'm at your command.'


At two o'clock displays started to zoom around the sky. Some solo, mostly in pairs and then a daring loop performance by a Tiger Moth. It was buttercup yellow with silver wings and Stacey knew that she had found the plane she wanted to fly.

Her brothers were allowed to explore by themselves, but Stacey wandered with her father amongst the high and low winged aircraft. Pilots chatted and held small children up to look into the cockpits.

The Tiger Moth was at the end of a row and Stacey impatiently dragged her father towards it. 'Look, Dad, it's the only one here. Quick! Before he leaves.'

Kevin Walsh, the pilot, leant against the fuselage. He was in his early sixties, tall and with a head of dark wavy hair. He had an almost square-shaped face roughened by the wind and sun.

'Hello, I'm Stacey Thompson. I was fourteen last week. Can I have a ride in your Tiger Moth?' The words spilled over each other and as she took a breath, Kevin turned to look at her.

Stacey smiled at him, knowing she could charm the devil if she wanted to.

'Well now, you're a bit young for my type of plane. It doesn't have covers over the cockpits and we would have to sit separately, you in the front and me behind. I'm sure your Dad would be very worried about you.'

'Dad won't worry. I'm tall for my age and ...'

'Definitely not, my girl. Your mother would have a fit. Sorry about this, but she's aeroplane mad. Pity my two boys aren't.'

Doug pulled Stacey away but she broke his hold and ran back to Kevin.

95

'Please, if I can't go for a ride, can I sit inside? I won't touch anything.'

'Is that OK with you, Dad?' Kevin asked.

'OK. Just a sit in.'

Kevin arranged the belts over her shoulders, explained the dials and controls.

'Tell you what young lady. When you reach eighteen come back and I'll give you a ride in the old Moth. I promise.'

'Dad, did you hear? I can come back for a ride.'

Doug shook Kevin's hand. 'Thanks a lot, you've made her day.'

\* \* \*

'Happy Birthday, Stacey. It's the big eighteen today.' Hilary Thompson hugged her tall, slim daughter and gave her a package.

Stacey ripped the silver paper from the box. Inside, cradled in yellow tissue paper lay a leather flying helmet and goggles. A card read: *For this weekend – have a great day.*

'Oh, Mum, they're beautiful. Dad has given me the air show ticket.'

A lump lodged in Stacey's throat. Her dream was about to come true.

For the past three years, Stacey and the family had gone to the air show and she had always talked to Kevin after his display. Although she only saw him at this annual event, her enthusiasm had sparked a kinship between them.

But over the past year the Thompson's had faced a crisis. Doug had been made redundant and money was tight. So this year Stacey was going alone.

Soon after the show opened, Stacey parked her 50cc scooter at Popstone Airfield. Little had changed since her first visit. The Control Tower and runway had been upgraded, but they still used rope barriers and the planes were paraded in rows.

After the display, Stacey searched for Kevin. She thought it strange that he hadn't been in the air. He wasn't in the parade area either.

Stacey felt frustrated. The outspoken, curly-headed teenager hadn't changed, even though she was now a young woman. She cherished this show day when she could talk mechanics, design and old planes with him.

She knew he kept the Moth in the hanger. Muttering to herself, hoping he was there, she set off across the field to find out. The doors were wide open.

The Tiger Moth was the only plane inside, parked at the back. It was quiet compared to the noise of the showground and as she walked further in it became much darker. She called Kevin's name. The Tiger Moth seemed in order, in fact, the plane looked ready for flight, but Kevin was nowhere to be seen.

Fingering her new leather helmet, Stacey's disappointment was all consuming. This was to be her special day, her special flight. Kevin had promised.

Out of the blue, Kevin was there, walking round from the other side of the plane.

'Are you ready, princess? Today's the day. We've waited a long time for this. I see Hilary bought what I suggested. There's a package in the front seat for you. Happy Birthday.'

Stacey eagerly opened her present. 'Wow, Kevin, a real leather flying jacket! Thanks a million.' She went to hug him, but he stepped back.

'My pleasure,' he laughed. 'Don't get any bigger, that cost me a whole day's worth of flying lessons.'

The fur lined jacket was a little too large, but strapped in her seat, helmet and goggles on, she felt just like Amy Johnson.

The noise of the engine was exhilarating as they flew up into the sky. Stacey marvelled at the green patchwork fields, threaded by streams. English country villages spread neat and picturesque. There was a cricket match and the players looked like pegs running between the wickets.

Climbing higher, Kevin asked through his mike, 'Would you like to loop, princess?'

'Oh, yes, please, high in the sky, over and over. This is wonderful.'

She felt the power, watched the altimeter rise and saw the world turn upside down. The grace of it was like a ballet as Kevin repeated the loops.

'Would you like to fly her?' His voice sounded like a whisper in her ears. 'You can't do much harm way up here.'

'Can I, just for a little while? You will watch what I'm doing? Take back the controls if I get into a dive?'

'Of course, but you'll be fine.'

Stacey placed her gloved fingers around the control stick and knew this was what she had always wanted – to fly. Above the summer countryside Stacey soared like a bird. She tried to remember all that Kevin had told her and as her natural talent took over, she felt as one with the Moth.

Kevin landed and taxied back to the same place in the hanger.

Standing beside the twin-winged Tiger Moth, Stacey smiled at Kevin. 'This has been the best day of my life.'

'A promise is a promise, princess. This was to be your day to fly. Take care of yourself. It's time for me to go.'

As Stacey walked out into the sun-soaked afternoon, she turned and waved – but he was gone.

She put her new flying jacket into the pannier of her scooter and stroked the soft leather. It was all hers, ready for the lessons she would have one day. As she reached for her crash helmet dangling from the handlebars, an announcement came over the loudspeaker.

*It is with regret that we have to announce the death of one of our pilots, Kevin Walsh, in a car accident on his way to the show today.*

Stacey froze, shocked and confused. 'But that's impossible,' she whispered. 'I've just been flying with him ...' Then she remembered his words from long ago.

'I promise.'

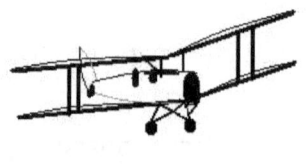

# ABOUT THE AUTHOR

I have been a 'writer' since I was fifteen years old. I loved my English literature lesson when we were told to write a composition.

Most times we were given a theme. But my favourite time was when I had a blank page and could write what I pleased; adventures in wild jungles, ancient castles, Cornish smugglers' coves. Capturing foreign spies and out-witting aliens from space.

Now, I write Romantic Historical novels set in the Georgian/Regency era – a dashing hero rescuing a spirited heroine from the wicked Spanish sea captain.

I am always looking for a challenge. My new Kaleidoscope series of short stories, will, I hope bring a smile or a tear as you read.

I am a member of the Romantic Novelists' Association. At their Golden Anniversary Conference year I was thrilled to achieve third place in the Elizabeth Goudge annual writing award.

Go to: http://accenthub.com/2016/12/1264466/
for an insight into my research and recent releases

You can find out more about my work at:

**www.julieroberts.me.uk**

**Facebook: @julieoroberts**

**Twitter: @julieoroberts**

# *Exclusive Extract*

As a thank you for purchasing this book, I am thrilled to share with you a further Exclusive Extract from my latest release: The Hidden Legacy.

I do hope that you enjoy it.

*Who is the mysterious Madame Lightfoot from Frederick's past?*

*

*On the death of her guardian, Frederick, Meredith Sanders inherits his art gallery in Ludgate Hill. This brings her closer to Blackfriars and Newgate Prison, the two places she most fears. Her ambition of becoming a renowned artist draws her into Frederick's criminal legacy and danger.*

*At first, businessman Adam Fox suspects Meredith of being involved in an art fraud relating to a missing Turner painting. Despite her fear of betrayal, she asks him for help as he is the only man she can trust.*

*If the painting is not returned to the Royal Academy before the Summer Exhibition, Adam may not be able to save her from the gallows.*

*And whatever her feelings for Adam, Meredith will not reveal the secrets of her own past...*

For readers of Nicola Cornick, and Stephanie Laurens, an exciting new voice in Regency romance.

**The story continues...**

# THE HIDDEN LEGACY

## CHAPTER ONE

### April 1815

Lead in ...

Meredith waited, her charcoal poised over the paper. Behind her she could feel Mr Fox's presence, caught the faint scent on his skin. Yet he was not threatening, instead there was a comfort in him being there. Her fingers relaxed and she studied the child. With quick strokes she drew the contours of her face, her lips, her nose, but it was her eyes sparkling with excitement that brought the sketch alive. Meredith finished the portrait with the tight fair curls peeking from under her cap and her shoulders covered with a lace collar.

Meredith turned and handed him her sketch book. Everything she hoped for now lay in Mr Fox's hand.

Read on ...

He stood silent. Then a smile parted his lips. It changed his countenance instantly. He glanced towards his niece and she started to rise, but he held up his hand. 'Sit a moment longer, Sarah. Patience is a lesson a young lady must acquire.' His tone was light but firm and the child sighed.

'I know, Uncle Adam.'

This was a different man to the one who had spoken so brusquely when he arrived. Was this a sign he was accepting her? The clock ticked away the minutes matching the thumping of her heartbeat as he studied the charcoal portrait.

'Miss Sanders, I am not a stickler for the high protocol of the gentry, but my niece is under my protection and I must be quite sure that she is brought up to a standard my brother-in-law would expect. Miss Weston is only eight years old, but I think she requires a younger person to be with for part of her education. Her day governess is a mature matron and very strict, a requirement my aunt insists on.'

What did this mean? Could she take this comment as an advantage? Waiting for his answer was a torture. She crossed her fingers, praying he would say yes. He went over to Frederick's portrait and studied it for several moments.

'May I offer a trial period of one month? If all progresses satisfactorily, then I see no reason why you should not continue Miss Weston's art tuition. I would insist, of course, on leaving a maid as her chaperone. Is this acceptable to you?'

Her breath left her in a rush. 'Thank you, Mr Fox. One month's trial and a chaperone are quite in order. Would you like to see the studio, sir?'

'I would indeed.' He turned his attention back to his niece. 'Come, Sarah, let us go and see Miss Sander's studio.'

The child who had waited with such patience now jumped up and down, her fair curls bobbing under her white cap. 'Oh, yes please, Uncle Adam.'

Meredith opened the door and stepped aside, allowing them to enter.

'Oh, this is so very nice. And there is paper and charcoal ready for me.' Miss Weston touched one of the four tables and sat down. 'Will I really be the only one?'

'At the moment, yes, but I hope to have other students very soon.'

Meredith's moment of optimism vanished as the child's forehead creased in a frown and Mr Fox started to tour the room as he had her gallery. The bareness of the room suddenly struck Meredith as a barrier; had he expected a more palatial room for his niece to study in?

Miss Weston's frown cleared and her face brightened as she asked, 'If I'm the only one, could you come to Tallow House? Then I can draw the garden.'

Mr Fox stopped pacing. 'Would you consider coming to Great Ormond Street, Miss Sanders?'

Go to his home! She didn't know anything about him. What if his motives were not honourable? 'I don't know how far ...' Her stomach was full of butterflies. She needed time to think, but this was not the time to go weak. 'I'm afraid not, sir. The cost of travelling and the time involved would not make it a viable business proposition for me.'

'Ah. So it is money that drives you, Miss Sanders. That I understand. May I make a proposal for your personal tuition of my niece? I will send my coach for you twice a week and provide all the materials you need and a room for a studio. Would double your fee cover the additional travelling time? If you wish to take on a little extra work, I will not object.'

He would not object! This was her business. She might be a woman in a man's world, but how dare he give out orders as though she were a servant? The superior manner of the man was ... She opened her mouth to say, 'No. Thank you,' but didn't. Twenty shillings a week, guaranteed, would give her a small income and pay Mrs Clements' wages. It left plenty of time to secure other clients and sell her paintings. And his disinterested approach didn't give the impression of any untoward intentions.

Squaring her shoulders to her full five feet six inches she looked into his dark eyes. 'I think I can agree to that, sir. When would you like Miss Weston to start?'

'Your advertisement read Monday and Wednesday. These are convenient days for me. I will send my coach at eight-thirty so you may start at nine o'clock. You will require paint and brushes and other supplies. My footman will call to collect a list this afternoon.'

In less than an hour, Mr Fox had taken over her professional tuition. And as for Miss Weston, she couldn't think why he had bothered to bring her; other than he was taking away her charcoal drawing.

But she replied. 'Yes, sir. I will agree to that.' Now was not the time to upset the apple cart and lose her only client.

Miss Weston was so excited she couldn't keep still and hopped from foot to foot, her fair curls bouncing with each hop. 'Thank you, Uncle Adam. Oh, I can't wait to paint like Miss Sanders.'

The man who had given her the chance to fulfil her dream stepped into the doorway. 'I have taken up most of your morning, so you may include today in your bill. Shall we say payment bi-weekly?'

Meredith felt she should stand to attention and salute, but his generosity deserved an appreciative reply. 'Thank you, Mr Fox. I'm sure Miss Weston and I will fare well together. I am confident you will see much improvement in her drawing and painting by the end of our trial period.'

She accompanied him through the gallery to the door. 'Thank you for your faith in me, Mr Fox.'

'I hope we will both benefit, Miss Sanders. Good day to you. Come, Sarah, Jackson will take you and Betsey home.'

Meredith saw Mr Fox speak to his coachman and, presumably, Betsey, the nursery maid standing beside the horses. A moment later, Miss Weston and her maid climbed into his coach and the rattle of the horses' harness faded as the coachman steered the two greys towards the city. Mr Fox walked away in the opposite direction to St Pauls.

Mr Fox was arrogant, but underneath this he had displayed kindness to both his niece and her. Wealth, however, did not give him the right to treat her as one of his servants – even though she did need his money.

Bright light blazed through a high window and sunshine filled the studio. The bareness of the walls had not seemed a disadvantage until Mr Fox started his inspection. Seeing it from a client's point of view, she needed a few of her paintings to add colour. And what better way to encourage students than by example – her watercolour landscape, the ruined castle in oil, she had charcoal and pencil drawings. Perhaps she should tell them painting didn't only go on paper and canvas – she had climbed a ladder with a bucket in one hand and a brush in the other and sloshed the whitewash on the walls. She wouldn't mention that her work apron didn't protect her dress, or her face and hands being spotted white.

Mr Fox intrigued her. Who was he? Definitely a gentleman of financial standing; but what business was he engaged in?

She glanced at her clock on the table, it showed eleven o'clock – only an hour left, but there was still time for the doorbell to tinkle again. She really did need one more pupil.

Meredith sat down at a table and stared at the blank sheet of paper. She picked up a charcoal stick and started to sketch Mr Fox: his dark hair, eyes black with sparks of white. His nose was firm and straight and the angular chin gave his face a determined expression. She remembered his indulgent smile to his niece and stroked the charcoal to form his mouth. Her gaze lingered on the parted lips. She wasn't sure her decision to give private lessons was a wise choice. What would have happened if she had asked for two pounds a week? Would Mr Fox have agreed? She most certainly needed to improve her negotiating skills.

At twelve o'clock, Meredith locked the front door. She was both elated and disappointed and just a little frightened that there had been no other client. She couldn't afford another advertisement until Mr Fox made his first payment. But she must be grateful to him, some money was better than none; after all, artists were renowned for being poor.

Meredith climbed the stairs to the first landing and stopped in the doorway of a square room that had been equipped as a kitchen. It overlooked the back yard and would be hot come summer, but today the warmth from the fire was most welcome.

Mrs Clements was a rotund woman and almost filled the space between the sink and table. She was straining water from a pot, the rising steam tinting her face a rosy red. Meredith loved the old lady, she was more than a paid servant, she was her dearest friend.

'Whatever you're cooking, Clemmie, it smells good. I need something nice to cheer me up.'

'Did you not fare well, dear?'

'I have one client and I agreed to go to his home to give private tuition to his niece.'

'Isn't that good?'

'Yes, but I will need to sell a painting before my next allowance.'

'Of course you'll sell one. Now, off you go into the parlour. I'll be five minutes. I have your favourite, boiled ham and bread.'

Meredith went back along the landing into a room with a window overlooking the busy shopping street. She leant her forehead on the glass and watched the stagecoach leave the Belle Sauvage and weave through the carriages that were vying for a place to stop. Doubts about the success of her venture plagued her again. The world of business was run by men; they made the rules. A spark of rebellion surged through her. She had challenged them before when a girl; she could do it now as a woman.

Clemmie came in and she turned round. All the furniture had come from Appleton House: the yellow brocade sofa from her bedchamber, the two brown wing chairs from Frederick's study, and the mahogany table and chairs from the dining room. The red and yellow carpet made it homely.

Inside this building she was safe, locked in a world provided for her by Frederick and because she had called herself Meredith Sanders from the day he found her.

Outside was the world she feared. She was caught between the two places that had haunted her for the past ten years – Newgate Prison and Blackfriars...

....................................................................

## Latest reviews of The Hidden Legacy:

This is no ordinary Regency Romance. It is so well researched and written that you feel you're there with the characters all the time. A very absorbing read that you couldn't put down. Well done Julie on your first book and I look forward to reading the next one! – Amazon reader

Meticulously researched, this story moves between the elegance and refinement of prosperous Regency London to a sinister criminal underworld full of threats and danger. A woman alone, determined to make her own way as an artist, Meredith is drawn into both worlds. Though he has his own reasons to distrust her, wealthy businessman, Adam Fox, joins her in a race against time to recover a missing Turner before the opening of the Royal Academy Summer Exhibition. This is a rollercoaster of a novel, an adventure shot through with issues of trust, love and loyalty. An engaging central couple and deftly woven back story makes this a great read – Hugh

Well written, language flows, although not my usual type of book, did enjoy it. – Amazon reader

Great book. Couldn't put it down. Characters were likeable and well developed and very in keeping with the time period it was set in. Can't wait for more by this author – Amazon reader

A perfectly pitched Regency romantic adventure. Engaging characters including a headstrong heroine, the right mix of historical background, romance, intrigue and skulduggery, and an interesting and unusual premise. I'll never visit an art gallery again without wondering! Well done, Julie Roberts, on her debut novel – Amazon reader

Once I started reading this book I couldn't put it down – Amazon reader

Very good book! I liked the story and the way it is written!! Romance, art, mystery and suspense are all in there! Couldn't stop reading it until the last page!!
Amazon reader

A really good read with an unusual plot. How refreshing to find a regency heroine with a skill and actually doing something to earn a living for a change. Well- paced right to the end and with interesting minor characters as well as a convincing relationship between the heroine and her man – Amazon reader

I've thoroughly enjoyed reading this book. The story draws you in and before you know it, you're turning the last page. Very much looking forward to the next book Julie publishes - hopefully I won't be waiting long!!
—Amazon reader

\*\*\*

Discover more about

The Hidden Legacy at:

https://www.accentpress.co.uk/the-hidden-legacy

# Regency Marriages Trilogy
# Book 2
# A Tangle of Secrets
# Out July 2018

*A circle of love, a forbidden marriage*

Read on ...

*Hannah Dudley is left impoverished in New York by her brother. One evening she finds a stranger, Christopher Forsythe, ill and dying on her doorstep.*

*Leaving him there will ensure his death.*

*Taking him in will ruin her reputation.*

*A marriage certificate will protect her.*


*Not even Hannah's devoted nursing can save Christopher. Months later, she receives an unforeseen letter from Christopher's brother, Lord Marcus. He offers, at the request of his mother, a place in their home in London.*

*Hannah is shocked to find she is now part of an aristocratic family. Reaching England, she finds the ton's social restrictions are difficult to deal with.*


*A forbidden love grows between Hannah and Marcus, even though they know the church will not sanction their marriage.*

*Hannah is faced with only one choice.*

*She must take a journey that will break her heart.*

*Leave Marcus and return to America ...*


**If these words have sparked your imagination, read A Tangle of Secrets, and their resolution**

*Julie*

www.ingramcontent.com/pod-product-compliance
Lightning Source LLC
Chambersburg PA
CBHW060643130626
46555CB00002B/928